Ka~~~
P~~~~ss

**Other books by
Ann M. Martin**

Leo the Magnificat
Rachel Parker, Kindergarten Show-off
Eleven Kids, One Summer
Ma and Pa Dracula
Yours Turly, Shirley
Ten Kids, No Pets
With You and Without You
Me and Katie (the Pest)
Stage Fright
Inside Out
Bummer Summer

For older readers:

Missing Since Monday
Just a Summer Romance
Slam Book

THE BABY-SITTERS CLUB series
THE BABY-SITTERS CLUB mysteries
THE KIDS IN MS. COLMAN'S CLASS series
BABY-SITTERS LITTLE SISTER series
(see inside book covers for a complete listing)

BABY-SITTERS
Little Sister

Karen's Snow Princess
Ann M. Martin

Illustrations by Susan Tang

A
LITTLE APPLE
PAPERBACK

SCHOLASTIC INC.
New York Toronto London Auckland Sydney

ISBN 0-590-06592-0

12 11 10 9 8 7 6 5 4 3 2 1   8 9/9 0 1 2 3/0

Printed in the U.S.A.   40
First Scholastic printing, February 1998

The author gratefully acknowledges
Stephanie Calmenson
for her help
with this book.

Karen's Snow Princess

It's Snowing!

It was early Saturday morning. I did not have to get up to go to school. I could stay in my bed and be snoozy and cozy. I did not even have to open my eyes. But I decided to take a peek when I heard something softly scraping against my window. I opened one eye and looked outside. Then both eyes popped open.

"Yippee!" I cried. "It is snowing!"

I ran to the window for a better look. It must have been snowing all night long. A soft white blanket covered everything in sight.

I was not the only one who had discovered the snow. My brother Andrew appeared at my door.

"It is snowing!" he said. "Let's go out and play!"

"Hurry and get dressed," I replied. "I will meet you outside."

Andrew is four going on five. That makes him my little brother, because I am already seven.

In case you are wondering, my name is Karen Brewer. I have blonde hair, blue eyes, and a bunch of freckles. I wear glasses. I have a blue pair for reading and a pink pair for the rest of the time. (I could see the snow without any glasses at all!)

In no time I was dressed and racing Andrew out the door.

The first thing we did was fall down on our backs in the snow and spread our arms and legs wide. We flapped them up and down. Then we stood up and saw two perfect angels on the ground.

"Now what?" asked Andrew.

"I know. Instead of making a snowman or a snowlady, let's make a snowcat," I said.

"Cool!" said Andrew.

"You are right. It will be a cool cat because it is made out of snow!" I said.

Andrew thought this was very funny. Even though he is little, he can be an excellent audience.

We were piling up snow for our snowcat's body when I heard someone tap, tap, tapping at a window. I looked up. Mommy was waving down to us. She smiled and opened the window a crack.

"Good morning!" she called. "You two are up early."

"We are making a snowcat!" I replied.

"A cool cat!" said Andrew.

"You will probably be hungry soon," said Mommy. "I will go downstairs and get breakfast ready."

I was glad. I was hungry already.

This morning there were just three of us at the little house. The three of us were Mommy, Andrew, and me. That is because Seth, my stepfather, was away for the weekend. Seth is a carpenter. He has been working on an important project in Chicago. He has been going there a lot on weekends.

Hold everything! I just told you I was at my little house. But I forgot to tell you I have a big house too. Do you want to know why? It is a long story. Are you ready? I will tell it to you now.

My Long Story

Ready? Set? Here comes my story!

It starts when I was very little. Back then I lived in a big house in Stoneybrook, Connecticut, with Mommy, Daddy, and Andrew. Then Mommy and Daddy started having troubles. They were fighting all the time. They tried hard to get along but just could not do it. Mommy and Daddy told Andrew and me that they loved each of us very much. But they did not want to be married anymore. So they got a divorce.

After the divorce, Mommy moved with

5

Andrew and me to a little house not too far away. Then she met Seth. Mommy and Seth got married. That is how Seth became my stepfather. So now when Seth is not traveling to Chicago, there are four people at the little house. They are Mommy, Seth, Andrew, and me. There are some pets too. They are Rocky, Seth's cat (he is a *real* cat, not a snowcat); Midgie, Seth's dog; Emily Junior, my pet rat; and Bob, Andrew's hermit crab.

Daddy stayed at the big house after the divorce. (It is the house he grew up in.) He met someone nice too. Her name is Elizabeth. She and Daddy got married. That is how Elizabeth became my stepmother.

Elizabeth was married before and has four children. They are my stepbrothers and stepsister. They are David Michael, who is seven like me; Sam and Charlie, who are so old they are in high school; and Kristy, who is thirteen and the best stepsister ever.

I have an adopted sister too. Her name is Emily Michelle. (I love her so much, I named my pet rat after her.) Emily is two and a half and came from a faraway country called Vietnam.

There is one more person who lives at the big house. That person is Nannie. She is Elizabeth's mother, which makes her my stepgrandmother.

Now for the big-house pets. They are Boo-Boo, Daddy's cranky old gray cat (he is *not* a cool cat!); Shannon, David Michael's big Bernese mountain dog puppy; Crystal Light the Second, my goldfish; and Goldfishie, Andrew's snowfish — I mean goldfish! Emily Junior and Bob live at the big house whenever Andrew and I are there.

Andrew and I switch houses almost every month. Now it is February and a little-house month. In March we will go back to the big house.

When Andrew and I switch houses, we do not have to take much with us. That is because we each have two of so many things. I even have special names for Andrew and me. I call us Andrew Two-Two and Karen Two-Two. (I got the idea from a book my teacher read us at school. It is called *Jacob Two-Two Meets the Hooded Fang.*)

Aside from two houses and two families, here are some other things we have two of: We each have two sets of toys, clothes, and books. I have two bicycles (one at each house), and so does Andrew. (I taught him how to ride a two-wheeler.) I have two stuffed cats. Goosie lives at the little house. Moosie lives at the big house. And I have two best friends. Nancy Dawes lives next door to the little house. Hannie Papadakis lives across the street and one house over from the big house. Nancy, Hannie, and I like to be together so much that we call ourselves the Three Musketeers.

"Ka-ren! An-drew!"

Mommy was calling us. But we were not finished with our snowcat.

"We will be there in a minute," I replied.

All we had left to do was give our snowcat a face. Andrew and I found some sticks and stones to make eyes, a nose, a mouth,

and whiskers. We arranged them just right.

"Meow," said Andrew.

"Brrr," I said. "I am cold. And hungry."

"Me too," said Andrew.

"We are on our way, Mommy!" I called.

And we ran inside for our breakfast.

An Important Announcement

As I walked in the door, the phone rang. It was Seth. Andrew and I each said a quick hello. Then we sat down to eat our breakfast. (Mommy wanted us to eat while it was hot. We were having oatmeal, toast, and cocoa.)

"Later we could make a snowmouse," said Andrew.

"Or snowkittens," I said.

Out of the corner of my eye, I noticed that

Mommy had turned away from us. She was whispering into the phone. She talked for a few more minutes, then hung up. She did not look happy.

"Is Seth okay?" I asked.

"Yes, he is fine," Mommy replied.

I was not so sure from the way she said it. But I could tell she did not want to talk about anything. She turned on the radio.

"Good morning! Thank you for tuning in to WSTO radio!" said the announcer's voice. "Here is your forecast for this bright white Saturday."

The steady snow was supposed to taper off into flurries.

"And now for a special WSTO community-service announcement," said the voice.

The minute I heard the words "special" and "announcement," I sat up tall. I *love* special announcements. My teacher, Ms. Colman, makes them sometimes. It usually means something exciting is going to happen.

"For those of you who have not yet

12

heard," said the announcer, "Stoneybrook is planning to hold a weeklong winter carnival. It will raise money to buy new equipment for our volunteer fire department. To kick off the festivities, there will be a First Night ceremony. That is a first for Stoneybrook."

"What is first? What is he saying?" asked Andrew.

"Shhh! We have to listen," I said.

The announcer explained that people all over town would decorate their trees and homes with lights. At an exact time to be announced on the radio, everyone would turn their lights on. At the same time there would be a lighting ceremony in the town square. The announcer told us to stay tuned for more exciting news. It was time for a commercial break.

"Wow! The whole town will be lit up like Christmas again!" I said while the commercials were on.

There were three commercials in a row. Then the announcer returned.

14

"We now have a prerecorded message from our very own Mayor Keane," he said.

I recognized the mayor's voice right away.

"First Night will be an exciting event in our town's history," she said. "To share the honor of this event, I will pick one citizen at random to pull the switch that will light our town square."

Omigosh! One person was going to light the town square! That would be a gigundoly great honor.

I closed my eyes and started wishing.

"Pick me, Mayor Keane," I whispered to myself. "Please, pick me to light the town square."

More Exciting News

Andrew did not understand exactly what was going on. I had to explain everything to him.

"We will go to the town square. The mayor will pick one special person to switch on the lights," I explained. (I did not tell Andrew that that person might possibly be me.)

"At the same exact time," I continued, "everyone at home will light up their trees and houses."

"How can we light up our house and be at the town square at the same time?" asked Andrew.

Hmm. This was an excellent question. I looked to Mommy for the answer. I hoped she was not going to say that we had to stay home. I could not do that. I had to be at the town square so Mayor Keane could pick me.

"You are right, Andrew. We cannot be in two places at once," said Mommy. "But there is something we can do. We can set a timer to turn on the lights while we are away."

Whew! That was a relief.

"Do we have a timer?" I asked.

"No, but we can get one. We need new lights too," said Mommy. "I have to pick up a few things downtown. Shall we go now?"

"Sure!" replied Andrew and I together.

We helped Mommy clean up the breakfast dishes. Then the three of us took a ride downtown to the hardware store. We can always find the things we need at Ted's Tools.

As we were walking into the store, Natalie Springer and her mother were walking out. Natalie is one of my classmates.

"Hi, Natalie!" I said. "What are you doing here?"

"We were getting lights for First Night," replied Natalie.

"That is what we are going to do now," I said.

"Did you read about the Snow Prince and Snow Princess contest?" asked Natalie. "I bet you want to be Snow Princess, right?"

"Well, I might if I knew what it was."

"The contest is part of the winter carnival. There is a flier about it inside the store. You can read all about it," said Natalie.

"Thanks!" I replied. "See you at school on Monday."

I found the flier posted by the cash register. While Mommy and Andrew were getting the things we needed, I read about the contest. These are the things I would have to do to become Snow Princess:

1. Write a 200-word essay on ways to improve Stoneybrook. Twenty semifinalists will be picked.

2. Give a five-minute speech about the winter carnival. Ten finalists will be picked.

3. Write and read aloud a 500-word composition beginning, "As Snow Prince (or Princess), I promise . . ." Two winners will be picked. They will be Stoneybrook's Snow Prince and Snow Princess!

I read the flier from start to finish. It said the winners would get to ride on a float in a parade.

Being Snow Princess sounded very cool. I am good at writing essays and compositions. And I am good at giving speeches. So I probably had a good chance of winning the contest if I entered it. But there was one big problem. I *really* wanted to light up the town square. If I were Snow Princess, I was sure the mayor would not pick me. After all, she could not let one person do *everything*.

Even if that one person were me, Karen Brewer.

I decided to stand back and let someone else be Snow Princess. Meanwhile I would keep wishing for the mayor to pick me to turn on the switch that would light up the town square.

I was making my wish again when Mommy and Andrew came to the cash register with three boxes of lights and a timer.

"Are you going to enter the contest?" asked Mommy when she saw the flier.

"No, I do not think so," I replied. "I have other plans."

The Election

On Monday morning at school, Ms. Colman picked me to take attendance. That is one of my favorite jobs. She handed me the attendance book and a blue pencil. I started checking off the names of everyone present.

First I checked my own name. Then I checked off Nancy and Hannie. (They sit all the way at the back of the room. I used to sit with them. Then I got my glasses and Ms. Colman moved me up front where I could see better.)

I checked the two other glasses-wearers next. They sit up front with me. They are Natalie and Ricky Torres. (Ricky is my pretend husband. We were married on the playground at recess one day.)

I checked off my best enemy, Pamela Harding, and her friends Jannie Gilbert and Leslie Morris.

Addie Sidney was putting snowman stickers on her wheelchair tray. (I wondered if she had a snowcat sticker. Probably not.) I checked off her name.

I checked off Bobby Gianelli, Hank Reubens, and Omar Harris. I checked Terri and Tammy Barkan. (They are twins.)

There were a few more names to check before I handed the book back to Ms. Colman.

"I am glad to see everyone is here," said Ms. Colman. "Now you will all have a chance to be in the election."

"Election! What election?" I cried.

Ms. Colman gave me her please-use-your-indoor-voice look.

"Sorry," I said. "What election are we having?"

"I have been asked to select a student to help in a kindergarten class once a week. I thought an election would be the fairest way to choose," Ms. Colman replied.

Everyone in class started talking at once. Ms. Colman clapped twice to get our attention.

"We will hold the election later this morning. You may take time now to prepare a short campaign speech. After you have given your speeches, we will vote," said Ms. Colman.

We all took out notebooks and pencils. I thought about being a kindergarten assistant. Being elected is always fun. But I did not really want this job. If I want to help a little kid, I can always help Andrew at home. Also, while I was visiting the kindergarten class, I might miss something important in Ms. Colman's room. I hate missing important events. So I decided to write a short and honest speech.

24

When my turn came I stood in front of the room and smiled the way politicians do on TV.

"Greetings, classmates," I said. "Helping kindergarten students is a very good thing to do. If I am elected, I promise to do a very good job. But I already have a little brother at home to help and would be happy to give the job to someone else. Thank you very much."

I bowed and returned to my seat.

"Thank you, Karen," said Ms. Colman.

She called on Natalie next. Natalie was bending down to pull up her socks. Natalie's socks are always drooping. When she stood up, I could see she was very nervous. Natalie is shy and does not like to speak in front of the class.

Natalie began her speech. She kept stopping to clear her throat. She lost her place a couple of times. Finally she got to the end.

"I would really, really like to be the kindergarten assistant. I hope you will elect me," she said.

She hurried back to her chair.

After everyone had had their turn to speak, we each wrote a name on a piece of paper. (I voted for Addie because I thought she gave the best speech.)

Then Jannie collected the votes and Ms. Colman counted them.

"The winner of the election is Omar Harris," said Ms. Colman. "Congratulations, Omar."

I heard someone let out a big sigh. It was Natalie.

Karen's Idea

Natalie was quiet during the rest of the morning. At lunch she ate just two bites of her sandwich. When the rest of us ran out to the playground, Natalie stayed behind. I could hear her crying. (Natalie snorts when she cries.)

"I will meet you later," I said to Hannie and Nancy. "I am going to talk to Natalie."

I sat down next to her.

"What is wrong?" I asked. "You have been unhappy all morning. Are you sad about the election?"

Natalie nodded.

"I did not win the election either," I said. "But I am not crying."

"But you have won other elections. I have never won any," Natalie replied. "No one likes me."

"I do," I said.

I said it mostly to make Natalie feel better. But sometimes I really do like her. It is true she is not the most fun person in the world. She worries too much. She cries too much. And she spends too much time pulling up her socks. But Natalie is nice. Someone needed to be nice back to her. I decided that someone should be me.

I thought of something nice to say.

"You won the Pizza Queen contest at Pizza Express," I said.

"They picked my name out of a barrel," said Natalie. "They did not *choose* me."

It was true. I could not remember Natalie ever being elected or chosen for anything. She did not know what it felt like to be a

winner. She needed to know. Suddenly I got a great idea.

"Remember the Snow Princess contest?" I said. "You should enter it."

"There is no way I could win a contest like that," said Natalie.

"Why not? You just have to write a few things and give a speech. You are a good writer," I said.

"I am tired of entering contests and losing. I would rather not enter at all," said Natalie.

"You do not know that you will lose. This time you could win. Especially if I help you," I said.

"Karen Brewer, you are a contest winner. I am a contest loser," said Natalie. "That is all there is to it."

Brring! Brring! The bell rang, ending recess.

I decided then and there to help Natalie be a contest winner. I would be her Princess Promoter. It was an important job. And I love important jobs!

When we returned to our desks, Ms. Colman asked us to take out our math books. In between math problems, I wrote Natalie notes.

The first note said, "The winner of the contest rides on a parade float. That winner could be *you*!"

The second note said, "Do not worry. I will help!"

I was writing my third note when Ms. Colman gave me a please-pay-attention look. I went back to my math.

I knew Natalie was not convinced yet. At least she was reading my notes. She was keeping an open mind.

"Being Snow Princess *could* be fun," she said on our way out of school.

"It would *definitely* be fun!" I said as I got on the school bus. "I will call you later!"

Natalie smiled. I could tell she liked having her very own Princess Promoter.

Mission Accomplished

When I returned home, Mommy had a snack waiting for Andrew and me. It was triangles of cinnamon toast with cream cheese and steaming cups of cocoa. Yum.

While we were eating, Seth walked in the door.

"Hooray!" I shouted.

Andrew and I ran to greet him. Seth gathered us into his arms for a three-way hug. Mommy joined us to make it four.

"I am so glad you are home!" I said.

"Me too," said Andrew.

"How was your trip?" asked Mommy.

"Very interesting," said Seth. "I will tell you about it later."

I wished he would tell us about it right away. But I did not say anything. I had something important to do. I had to call Natalie. If we were going to enter her in the contest, we had to get started on the essay right away.

I dialed Natalie's telephone number.

"Hi, Natalie. It is me, Karen," I said. "Are you ready to write your first essay?"

"I am still not sure I want to enter the contest, Karen," Natalie replied. "I do not know what to say in my essay. I do not know how to improve Stoneybrook."

Just then I got another great idea.

"Natalie, I will call you right back. Do not go away," I said.

I hung up the phone and looked for Seth. I told him about the contest and how Nat-

33

alie needed to win it to improve her confidence.

"Do you think you could drive us around Stoneybrook this afternoon? I am sure if we rode around town, Natalie would find plenty of things to write about in her essay," I said.

"I was going to work at my studio. But I can do that tonight. Spending time with you is much more important," said Seth. "I will be happy to drive you and Natalie around town."

"Can I come too?" asked Andrew.

"You sure can," replied Seth.

I called Natalie back. I told her we would pick her up in ten minutes.

"I still do not know if I want to enter," said Natalie.

"I am not worried," I replied. "Once you see how much there is to write about, I am sure you will change your mind."

I was right. On our ride around town, we saw lots of trouble spots. We made a list of the things we saw:

34

ONE CROOKED STOP SIGN
A broken window at the post office
A TREE KNOCKED DOWN IN A STORM THREE WEEKS
AGO
Two overflowing garbage cans right in the
town square.

"What do you think about entering the contest now?" I asked when we dropped Natalie off at her house.

"You were right," Natalie replied. "There is a lot that needs to be done in this town. And I am going to write about it!"

Hooray! Mission accomplished. Well, almost. Natalie was going to enter the contest. Now all I had to do was help her win.

Karen Brewer, Teacher

That night I called Natalie again.

"How is your essay coming along?" I asked.

"I have only four sentences. I cannot think of what to say," replied Natalie.

"Write two more sentences. I will help you tomorrow at recess," I said. "And maybe you can come over after school."

When I hung up the phone, I thought of all the things I would say if it were *my* essay. My essay would be as long as a book. I would just have to show Natalie how to do it. I would have to be her teacher.

The next day at recess, Natalie and I stayed in the lunchroom to work on her essay. This is what she had written:

There are many troubles in the town of Stoneybrook. Here are the things I saw:

One crooked Stop sign

A broken window at the post office

A tree knocked down in a storm three weeks ago and

Two overflowing garbage cans right in the town square.

We should fix these things very soon. Thank you.

"Your essay is too polite," I said. "It needs more feeling. Don't you feel mad about these things?"

Natalie nodded.

"Then let the judges know," I said. "Write a sentence about how mad you are."

Natalie wrote, "I am very mad about these things."

"You need more feeling," I said. "How about, 'These things are terrible! They are awful. I am so mad, I could spit.' "

"Um, Karen, I am not really that mad," said Natalie.

"But you have to write that you are. It makes the essay better," I replied.

Natalie added a couple of sentences.

"Now you have to tell the town what to do about the troubles," I said.

"I do?" said Natalie.

I sighed. "We have a lot more work to do. I am glad you are coming over later."

After school we had a snack, then went up to my room to work on the essay. We worked until Natalie's mother picked her up.

"I will call you later," I said.

I called right after dinner and we worked on the essay some more.

We worked the next day at recess and again after school. Finally the essay was finished. But it was written on a sloppy piece of paper with lots of crossing out.

38

"It has to look neat," I said.

"I will copy it over tonight and bring it to school tomorrow to show you," said Natalie.

The next day I looked at Natalie's essay. I had forgotten that Natalie's handwriting was messy no matter how hard she tried to be neat. She crossed her *l*s so they looked like *t*s. And her *n*s had an extra bump so they looked like *m*s.

I made her write it again while I looked over her shoulder. When she finished, it was much neater.

"Do you have a flower stamp for the envelope?" I asked.

"Do you think that matters?" said Natalie.

"Of course it does! If you want to win the contest, everything has to be perfect!"

"I will get a flower stamp," said Natalie. "But I will probably lose anyway."

"That is no way to talk," I said. "You have to have confidence."

That night Natalie called to tell me she

had mailed the essay with a yellow rose stamp on the envelope.

"Thanks for helping, Karen," she said.

"No problem. It was fun," I replied.

I meant it. Being Karen Brewer, Teacher, was fun. Maybe I will be a teacher when I grow up.

So Far, So Good

The following Saturday I got a phone call from Natalie.

"I just opened my mail. I got a letter from the contest committee. It says I am one of the twenty semifinalists," said Natalie.

"Congratulations! That is great!" I replied.

"Thanks," said Natalie.

"You do not sound very excited. Is something wrong?"

"I am happy to have won. But maybe *I* did not really win the contest. Maybe *you* are the real winner," said Natalie.

"No way," I replied. "You are the winner for sure. I only helped you."

"I guess so. Well, anyway, I just thought you would want to know about the letter."

"We should celebrate," I said. "Maybe we could go to the Rosebud Cafe for ice-cream sundaes."

"I do not feel like celebrating," Natalie replied. "I will see you at school on Monday."

"Wait! We have to work on the next part of the contest. You have to write a speech."

"I will think about it. I am not sure I want to be in the contest anymore."

"You have to stay in it to be the Snow Princess," I said.

"I will let you know on Monday," replied Natalie. "I have to go now, Karen. 'Bye."

Natalie hung up the phone. I wondered if I would have to convince her all over again on Monday. Oh, well. I was not going to worry about that now. It was time to celebrate. Even if Natalie did not think so.

I ran to find Mommy and Andrew, and I

told them the good news. Since Seth was in Chicago again, I asked, "Mommy, can we call Seth now? Please?"

I wanted to tell him the news very badly. He was the one who had driven Natalie and me around town so we could write the essay. I knew he would be happy.

"I am sorry," Mommy replied. "Seth has an important meeting this morning. He said he would call us later. You can give him the good news then."

"But I want to talk to him now. Could we interrupt his meeting for just a minute? I will talk very fast."

"That would not be a good idea," said Mommy. "When he calls later, I will let you be the first to talk to him."

"I want to be first to talk!" said Andrew.

"You cannot be first!" I said. "You do not have important news. I do."

"I do have important news. I am the cookie monitor at school!" said Andrew.

"That is not as important as Natalie winning the essay contest."

"It is too important."

"It is not!"

"Karen and Andrew. Please stop arguing," said Mommy. "Andrew, I promised Karen she could talk to Seth first this time. Next time you can talk first."

Boo. I did not like when Seth traveled so much. If Seth were around, Andrew and I would not be arguing. We both just wanted Seth to come home.

Coach Karen

On Monday morning at school I got good news. Natalie had decided to stay in the contest.

"But I want to write the speech by myself," she said.

"Are you sure? Don't you want even a little help from me?"

"No, I do not. I can only feel like a real winner if I write the speech myself."

My feelings were a little hurt, but I understood.

"Can I at least help you practice giving

the speech?" I asked. "I will not help too much. Only a little, I promise."

"I guess that will be all right. Even if you help me practice, I will still be the one who gives the speech. So I would still be the real winner."

The next day Natalie brought her speech to school. I read it at recess. It was pretty good. (It was messy, but that did not matter. The judges were not going to see it.)

It was time to begin my new job as Coach Karen.

"Remember, writing a good speech is only half your job," I said. "The other half is presenting it well. I will be your speech coach. Are you ready for your first speaking tip?"

"I guess so," said Natalie. She was already starting to look nervous.

"Number one, no drooping socks. I will lend you a non-droopy pair. Just tell me what color you want."

"Um, I do not know. I guess I will wear my nicest outfit. That is a blue jumper and a white turtleneck," replied Natalie.

"I will give you a pair of blue socks," I said. "Tip number two, stand up straight. You are drooping like your socks."

Natalie tried standing up straight. She looked very uncomfortable.

"You have to look more relaxed," I said.

Natalie relaxed. That made her droopy again.

"We will practice that tomorrow," I said. "Next tip — speak loudly and clearly."

"I will," Natalie mumbled.

"I cannot hear you!"

"I said, 'Okay!' " Natalie shouted.

I covered my ears. "Shouting is no good. I am sure judges do not like to be shouted at."

Brring! Brring! Natalie was saved by the bell. It was the end of recess.

"I will call you tonight with more important tips," I said.

That night when I called, I was holding a list. I read the list tip by tip.

"You need at least eight hours of sleep every night from now on," I said. "You will

48

need to clean your glasses so they sparkle. Do you have a blue hair barrette? If not, I will lend you one. And do not forget to smile a lot. That is important."

It was an excellent list of tips. I do not think Natalie could have found a better coach than me.

And the Winner Is . . .

The speaking contest was held at the Stoneybrook Public Library the following Saturday. I made sure Mommy, Andrew, and I were there early to get good seats. (Seth was in Chicago again for the weekend. Boo.)

Natalie arrived with her parents.

"Hi!" I called. "You look great!"

She really did. Her socks were not drooping. Her glasses were shiny clean.

"Do you need any last-minute tips?" I asked.

50

"I do not think so. I have practiced a lot. I feel ready," Natalie replied.

"Good luck," I said. I gave her the thumbs-up sign.

Natalie sat behind the podium with the other contestants. I knew a few of the kids from school and the neighborhood. We waved to each other.

Then Ms. Feld, the children's librarian, walked to the front of the room. I love Ms. Feld. I smiled at her.

"Thank you all for coming," she said, smiling back. "As you know, the money we earn from the sale of tickets to the winter carnival will go to our volunteer fire department and to the town of Stoneybrook. We thank you for your support. And now, let me present the first of our speakers, Bill Korman."

Bill is nine. He lives across the street from the big house. He was all dressed up in a jacket and a tie. He walked to the podium and gave his speech. It was very good. Maybe he would be the Snow Prince.

Ms. Feld introduced the next speaker.

"We will now hear from Natalie Springer," she said.

Suddenly I felt butterflies in my stomach. I was a nervous coach.

Natalie walked to the podium looking very serious. She needed to relax and smile. I tried to catch her eye. When she saw me, I put a big smile on my face. Natalie got the idea. She took a deep breath, smiled, and began.

"I would like to tell you what the winter carnival means to me," she said. "In winter, people can become lonely. They might stay indoors because it is too cold to go out. But a good cause brings people together. Helping our volunteer fire department is a very good cause."

Natalie talked about a fire in our town and how the firefighters came quickly and saved lives.

"They are there when we need them. Having this winter carnival shows them we are there when they need us. It is cold outside, but we will stay warm together. Thank you."

Wow! Natalie did a great job. And guess what? She won! She was chosen to be one of the ten finalists.

Natalie ran to hug her parents, then she ran to me.

"I am a winner! Thank you, Karen!" she said. "I feel like a *real* winner too, because I wrote and presented the speech myself. But I could not have done it without you."

I was gigundoly proud. I was glad Mommy and Andrew were there to see Natalie. I wished Seth could see too. I would tell him everything when he called. But it would not be the same.

I could not understand why he was away so much. He and Mommy had so many secrets lately. They were not fighting, so I did not think they were getting a divorce. But something was going on and I did not know what it was. I did not like that at all.

When Seth called after lunch, I told him about Natalie.

"That is great news," said Seth. "I am surprised you do not sound happier."

"I am not happy," I replied. "You are away too much."

"I do not *want* to be away so much," replied Seth. "But this project is very important. I will probably have to be away next weekend too."

"But you will miss First Night," I said. "Can't you stay home? Please?"

"I am so sorry, Karen. We will talk about this more when I get home. I promise," he said.

I felt awful. Seth would not get to see me light up the town square. Lately Seth was not around to see anything.

Karen to the Rescue

Natalie was ready for the final stage of the Snow Princess contest. I was ready too. I called her that night.

"Do you want to get together tomorrow to work on your composition?" I asked.

"No, thank you. I would rather work on it alone," Natalie replied.

"Well, you did a good job writing your speech. I am sure you will write a very good composition," I said.

I was not as sure as I sounded. And I did not want to take any chances with the contest. Natalie needed to win more than ever. That is because her hopes were up now. If she lost, she would feel doubly bad.

I called Natalie the next morning.

"How are you doing with your composition?" I asked. "Do you want to read it to me?"

"I am still writing it, Karen."

"That is okay. You can read what you have written so far."

"Oh, all right. But we cannot stay on the phone long. I have to finish," Natalie replied.

Natalie read the title, "As Snow Princess, I Promise . . ." Then she read what she had written.

I was glad she was going to work on it more. So far it did not sound like a prize-winning composition to me. But I tried to be encouraging.

"It is a good start," I said. "You can give it to me when you finish and I will look it over for you."

"I do not know. I really want to do this myself, Karen."

"Even real authors have editors," I said. "I will just check to see if there are spelling mistakes or anything."

"Well, maybe. I will let you know tomorrow."

By the end of school the next day, Natalie finally agreed to let me look at her composition. I took it home and went straight to my room to read it.

It was better than it had been. In fact, it was pretty good. But it was still not good enough. I fixed some spelling mistakes. I added a missing period.

Then I changed a couple of words at the beginning. I did not think Natalie would mind. The new words made her composition sound much better.

I changed a few more words. Then I took out a couple of Natalie's sentences and put in my own.

The composition was getting better with

every change. There was only one problem. It was not exactly Natalie's composition anymore. I was not sure I should change anything else. But there was one other part that would be so easy to fix. I could not resist. Finally, I rewrote the composition from the beginning. I drew a few pictures too.

The contest rules said the composition had to be in the mail by midnight. I had promised Natalie I would mail it for her. I copied it over carefully, addressed the envelope, and put on a rose stamp. Then I took the envelope to the corner mailbox.

My stomach did a flip-flop. Before I dropped the envelope in, I had to think. I had made a lot of changes. But how could it hurt to make Natalie's composition better? I just wanted to be sure she would be the winner. Natalie Springer, Snow Princess. How could she mind?

Oops

The ten finalists were invited to read their compositions on Wednesday afternoon at the library.

I went with Natalie and her parents. That is because Mommy was at home with Andrew, who had a cold. And Seth was at work in his studio. (At least he was back in Stoneybrook.)

Natalie was the third finalist called on to read. I could see she was feeling good. She was standing up tall, her socks were not drooping, and she was smiling.

Ms. Feld handed her the composition the judges had received.

"We enjoyed reading your composition very much. We also liked the beautiful illustrations," said Ms. Feld.

Natalie looked a little puzzled. I had not told her I illustrated the composition when I copied it over. In fact, I had not even told her I copied it over.

"Thank you," said Natalie.

Without looking in my direction, she began to read.

"As Snow Princess, I promise to do many exciting and important things for the town of Stoneybrook."

Natalie was still smiling, but her smile was a little shaky. She had not expected the words "exciting and important" in her composition. I had added them.

"The Snow Princess must stand for many things," continued Natalie. "I promise to be cheerful and friendly. I will work with my loyal Snow Prince to make Stoneybrook a fairy-tale town."

Natalie's eyes opened wide. That whole paragraph must have been a big surprise. She had not written one word of it.

Natalie swallowed hard and continued reading as if nothing were wrong. But at the end, she started to look a little wobbly.

"I promise I will try gigundoly hard to be the best Snow Princess this town has ever had."

When she finished speaking, the audience clapped. Natalie was smiling, but she did not look happy.

For the first time since she started speaking, Natalie looked in my direction. She gave me a big what-have-you-done-now look. Oops.

Princess Who?

We listened to the rest of the speakers. Then everyone was invited to have juice and cookies while the judges made their decisions.

I did not feel much like eating. And I thought it would be better for me to leave Natalie alone. I went to the bathroom and washed my hands and combed my hair six times.

I returned to the conference room when I heard Ms. Feld say, "Please take your seats, everyone. We are ready to name the Snow

Prince and Snow Princess for our winter carnival."

We all sat down quickly and Ms. Feld continued.

"First, we want to congratulate each of our speakers for doing a wonderful job. We thank you for contributing your time and ideas," she said.

We clapped for the contestants. Then Ms. Feld announced the first winner.

"Based on his fine composition, the judges name Bill Korman Snow Prince of the winter carnival," said Ms. Feld. "Congratulations, Bill."

I clapped for my big-house neighbor as he stepped forward to accept his crown and certificate of honor. He had done a very good job. I could see he was happy to have won.

When the room was quiet again, Ms. Feld continued. She was ready to name the Snow Princess. I crossed all my fingers and wished as hard as I could for my friend to win.

"Based on her wonderful composition, we name Natalie Springer Snow Princess of the winter carnival," said Ms. Feld. "Congratulations, Natalie."

"Yes!" I shouted. "Hooray!"

I jumped out of my seat and clapped louder than anyone in the room. Until I saw Natalie's face. It was not the face of a winner. It was not the face of a happy Snow Princess. It was a confused face. I stopped clapping and sat down again.

After thanking the judges and shaking their hands, Natalie walked toward the audience. Her parents were waiting to congratulate her. They were thrilled that their daughter had been named Snow Princess.

"Would you please excuse me for a minute?" she said to them. "I would like to talk to Karen in private."

I followed Natalie down the hall. Her lower lip started to quiver. That always happens to Natalie when she is upset.

"Please do not cry," I said. "I know you are unhappy with me. But you should be happy for yourself. You are Snow Princess! You won the contest and you should be proud."

"Why should I be proud?" asked Natalie. "Ms. Feld said I was chosen based on my wonderful composition. Only it was not my composition. It was *yours*. Now what am I supposed to do?"

"You are supposed to enjoy being Snow Princess."

"I cannot enjoy something I do not deserve. I feel like a cheater, even though I did not do anything wrong."

Natalie sounded angry and I could not blame her. Because of me, she would not enjoy being Snow Princess. Because of me, Natalie felt like a cheater.

I knew there was only one thing to say, and I said it: "Natalie, I am really sorry."

The Real Story

I called Natalie after supper that night. I had done a lot of thinking.

"Here are our choices," I said. "You can be the Snow Princess and not tell anyone I changed your composition."

"We already decided that is dishonest. I cannot do it," replied Natalie. "What other choices do we have?"

"I could only think of one. We can tell the truth."

"I like that one. We can tell Ms. Feld. She can talk to the other judges."

The next day after school Natalie's mother drove us to the library. (We told Mrs. Springer we needed to ask Ms. Feld some questions about being Snow Princess. It was sort of the truth.)

Ms. Feld was happy to see us.

"Welcome, Karen. And welcome, Natalie, our new Snow Princess," she said.

"We need to talk to you about that," said Natalie.

"I will be happy to answer any questions you have."

For a minute Natalie and I just stood there looking at each other. We had not decided who would do the talking.

Then Natalie blurted out, "I should not be Snow Princess! Karen wrote my composition. But I did not know that she did it."

Ms. Feld looked confused. I decided it was my turn to talk, since the whole mess was my fault. I explained everything. I told Ms. Feld how I got carried away and rewrote the composition to help Natalie win.

"I was trying to be a good Princess Pro-

moter," I said. "I wanted Natalie to win very badly."

"Natalie, do you still have the composition you wrote yourself?" asked Ms. Feld.

"Yes," replied Natalie. "But it is my first copy and it is very messy."

"That is okay," said Ms. Feld.

Natalie handed the composition to Ms. Feld.

"I will read this carefully and discuss it with the other judges. I promise to call you later this evening," said Ms. Feld.

We thanked Ms. Feld, then headed outside. I saw Natalie's lip begin to quiver. I was afraid she was going to start crying.

"Do you want me to keep you company until you get the phone call tonight?" I asked.

"Would you?" asked Natalie. "I really do not want to be alone. You could have dinner at my house."

"I will call home and see if it is all right. There is a phone right over there," I said.

I did not want to be away from Seth. I

hardly got to see him because he was in Chicago so much. But I decided it was important for me to be with Natalie. She was afraid to wait for this phone call without a friend. And I did not want her to be all alone if they took away her crown.

Omigosh! They might take away Natalie's crown. That would be even worse than not winning in the first place. It would be worse than losing the class election.

Maybe I was not such a good Princess Promoter after all.

The Real Princess

Mommy and Seth said I could have dinner at Natalie's house. I explained that she was upset and needed my company.

That part was the truth. Natalie was upset. But she was not the only one. I was upset, too.

At Natalie's house, Mrs. Springer offered us a snack. She made toast with peanut butter and honey and warm apple cider.

But Natalie and I were not hungry. We nibbled corners of the toast and took little sips of cider.

"Are you girls all right? Would you like something else to eat?" asked Mrs. Springer.

"No, thank you. We are not very hungry," I said.

We excused ourselves and went upstairs. We did not feel like playing either. We sat on Natalie's bed and watched her pet mouse, Delroy. He was running along a wheel in his cage. We watched the wheel go round and round.

Ring! When the phone rang, Natalie and I both tumbled off the bed.

"I bet it is Ms. Feld! She is calling early!" I said.

"Mommy, is that for me?" called Natalie.

"No, Natalie," answered Mrs. Springer.

"I am feeling very jumpy," I said. "I think we should take a walk."

We bundled up because it was cold outside. At the bottom of the Springers' driveway, Natalie turned left. I turned right. We smashed into each other.

"Oops, sorry," I said.

I turned and started to walk left. Natalie

turned and started to walk right. Now we were walking away from each other.

"I do not think we should go for a walk after all," I said. "What if Ms. Feld really does call early? We do not want to be out."

"You are right!" said Natalie. We hurried back into the house. Mrs. Springer was off the phone.

"What is going on with you, girls?" she asked. "I have never seen you so jumpy."

Natalie and I looked at each other. It was time to tell our story again. When we finished, Mrs. Springer said, "Karen, I know you were trying to do something nice for Natalie when you rewrote the composition. So do not feel too bad. And Natalie, even if you are not the Snow Princess, we love you anyway."

Telling the truth always seems to work the best.

Natalie and I were feeling a little less jumpy. By dinnertime our appetites were back. We helped Mrs. Springer make a big salad. Then Mr. Springer came home with pizza from Pizza Express.

"I am glad you girls are hungry. I got extra large pies tonight," he said.

Ring! We were just finishing our dinner when the phone rang again. This time it was for Natalie. Ms. Feld was calling with the judges' decision. I listened to Natalie talking on the phone.

"Really? You mean it?" said Natalie. "Thank you! Thank you very much!"

When she hung up, I said, "What happened? What did Ms. Feld say?"

Natalie was beaming.

"Ms. Feld said the judges liked your composition very much. It was definitely a prizewinner. But they liked my own composition even better!" said Natalie. "They are doubly sure they picked the right princess. Can you believe it? I am the Snow Princess. The *real* princess!"

"Congratulations! That is great!" I said.

My feelings were a teensy bit hurt when I

heard that the judges liked Natalie's composition better than mine. But it was for a worthy cause.

Natalie had finally been chosen for something important. And the best part was that she had been chosen just for being Natalie.

Seth's News

That night, I told Mommy and Seth about Natalie and the composition.

"I am glad everything worked out," said Mommy. "And I am glad you told us what happened. Having too many secrets is not good."

"You and Seth have been keeping lots of secrets lately," I replied.

"You are right, Karen," said Seth. "I promised to tell you what has been going on, and this is a good time."

Mommy called Andrew. We all went into

the den. I was feeling nervous. I was afraid I was going to hear bad news.

"What is going on?" asked Andrew.

"I want to tell you why I have been going to Chicago so much lately," replied Seth. "I have been going there because I was offered a temporary job."

Andrew looked confused.

"Temporary means it will not be for always," said Mommy. "This job would be for six months."

"Six months? That is a very long time!" I said.

"We have not made a decision yet," said Seth. "But it is an exciting offer and I would like to consider it."

"Wouldn't you miss us if you moved away for six months?" I asked.

"Of course," replied Seth. "That is why we would move there together."

My stomach did a flip-flop. Now I understood. Mommy and Seth were thinking of moving us all to Chicago.

"I do not want to move!" I said.

"Me either," said Andrew.

"It would not be forever," said Mommy.

"How can I see Daddy and everyone at the big house when we are far away?" I asked.

"How could I go to school?" asked Andrew.

"You would both come back for weekends sometimes," said Mommy. "And you would go to new schools in Chicago."

I did not like the sound of this one bit. Seth must have seen how unhappy I looked.

"If moving seems too difficult, I would consider commuting," said Seth.

Andrew looked confused again.

"Commuting means going back and forth," I told Andrew. "That is what Seth is doing now."

"But I would do it for a much longer time," said Seth.

"This is a lot to think about," said Mommy. "We do not have to decide anything right now. We just wanted to let you know what was going on."

I was relieved to know what the whispering was about. I had been worried about the secrets. But now I had an even bigger worry. I had to worry about moving to Chicago.

I did not want to leave my big-house family. I did not want to leave my friends and my school.

But I did not want Seth to commute either. I was not happy when he was away so much.

There was only one thing I wanted. I wanted Seth to turn down the job so we could all stay right where we were.

First Night

My little-house family ate breakfast to-gether on Saturday morning. Then we said good-bye to Seth. He was going to go to Chicago for the whole week.

"I will be back in time for the end of the carnival so I can go to the parade with you," he said. "And I will call you later to hear all about First Night."

I had been worrying so much lately about Natalie and Seth that I had almost forgotten about the lighting ceremony. I started think-ing about it again. I wanted Mayor Keane to choose me to light the town square. By the time Seth called, I wanted to have exciting news to tell him.

It was hard waiting for the afternoon to come. The ceremony did not start until four-thirty. I had to find things to keep me busy.

First Mommy, Andrew, and I hung our new lights. Then we set the timer and tested it. It worked! At five o'clock in the afternoon, our house would glow.

I made some phone calls. I called Hannie and Nancy and Natalie. I called my big-house family. (They would be at the ceremony too. That meant they would see me light the town square if I got picked.)

I ate lunch. I read a book. Then I planned what to wear. That was important. If I wanted the mayor to pick me out of the crowd, I had to be sure she could see me. I propped Goosie up on my bed.

"It is time for a fashion show," I said.

I pulled out all my sweaters. My yellow sweater was the brightest. It popped out from all the rest. The yellow turtleneck popping out of my bright red ski jacket was just what I needed.

Then I remembered something else I needed. One of my Christmas gifts had been a baseball cap with lights that blinked. I searched my closet until I found it. I tried out the lights. They worked. The mayor was sure to see me in my yellow sweater and blinking hat.

But I was not taking any chances. I went to my night-table drawer and took out one more thing. A flashlight. By the time the ceremony began, it would be almost dark. A flashlight was just what I needed. I would wave it in circles. There was no way the mayor could miss me with a red jacket, yellow sweater, blinking hat, and waving light.

"Karen! It is almost time to go," called Mommy.

Finally. We drove downtown and parked. The town square was packed with people. But that was okay. I did not need to be at the front of the crowd. I knew the mayor would find me wherever I was.

She stepped up to the microphone. The ceremony was about to begin!

"Welcome to our First Night ceremony," said Mayor Keane. "As you know, this begins our weeklong winter carnival. All ticket and prize money will go to help our volunteer fire department and to beautify our town. And now, to start the carnival, I am going to ask one of you to flip the switch that will light up our town square."

The mayor looked out at the crowd. The sun was just dipping down behind a building. The sky was turning gray. So was the crowd. Except for me. In my yellow sweater and blinking cap, and with my spinning light, I stood out. The mayor could not miss me. She was looking my way. She was pointing. She had found me!

"Please come up and light our town square," she said.

For a minute I thought I must be dreaming. Then Mommy said, "Go on, Karen. The mayor has chosen you."

Yippee! I had been picked to light the

town square. The crowd grew very quiet as I walked to the mayor. She shook my hand then told me what I needed to do.

First I turned and waved to the crowd. (The mayor did not tell me to do that. I thought of it by myself.) Then I turned around and flipped the switch.

I heard oohs and ahs. Then everyone in town began clapping. I had made Stoneybrook glow. Later, when Seth called, I would have exciting news to tell him.

A Winter Carnival Play

On Monday at school Ms. Colman made a Surprising Announcement (my favorite kind).

"Since this is winter-carnival week, we will do one thing each day to raise money for the town. Any suggestions?" she asked.

My hand shot up first. Ms. Colman called on me.

I shared my ideas with my classmates. I had lots of them.

"To raise money for our town, I think we

should have a walk-a-thon, sell homemade firefighter hats, have a class penny jar, put on a play —"

"Hold on, Karen. Give your classmates a chance," said Ms. Colman.

Almost everyone had a good idea. Ms. Colman made a list. I was happy that my ideas for the play and the class penny jar were at the top of the list.

We worked on our play all week long. We put it on at school on Friday afternoon. People had to buy tickets to see our play, and we raised almost a hundred dollars.)

The play was called *Help! Fire!* I was the narrator. I got to be on stage during the entire play. Here is our script:

Help! Fire!

Narrator: Act One of our play begins three weeks before the winter carnival. It takes place at a pizza parlor.

Pizza Maker: Good afternoon. What kind of pizza would you like today?

Customer Number One: I would like a large pizza with extra cheese and pepperoni, please.

Pizza Maker: One large pizza coming right up.

Narrator: The pizza maker tossed the dough. She covered it with sauce, cheese, and pepperoni. She put it in the oven to bake.

Customer Number Two: Sniff, sniff. Something is burning.

Pizza Maker: Sniff, sniff. You are right!

Customers and Pizza Maker: Help! Fire!

Narrator: Everyone ran outside. The pizza maker called 911 from a phone booth. The emergency operator called the Stoneybrook Volunteer Fire Department. Everyone waited and watched. The firefighters took a long time to come. Finally they arrived on foot. By then the pizza parlor had burned to ashes.

Pizza Maker: What happened? We called you hours ago.

Firefighter Number One: Our old fire truck

broke down. There was nothing we could do. I am sorry.

Narrator: End of Act One. Act Two takes place at a bakery a week after the winter carnival.

Baker Number One: What kind of pies shall we make today?

Baker Number Two: Let's make apple pies. Our customers love them!

Narrator: They made the crust, cut the apples, added sugar, and popped the pies into the oven.

Baker Number One: Sniff, sniff. I smell smoke!

Baker Number Two: Sniff, sniff. Our bakery is on fire!

Narrator: The bakers ran outside and called 911. The emergency operator called the Stoneybrook Volunteer Fire Department. In no time the firefighters arrived at the scene. *Whoosh!* They put out the fire.

Baker Number One: You saved our bakery!

Baker Number Two: How did you get here so fast?

Firefighter Number One: We have a brand-new fire truck that never breaks down. It was bought with money raised at the winter carnival. Thank you, Stoneybrook!

Narrator: You are welcome, firefighters. Thank you for being brave and saving lives. And thank you, audience. We hope you enjoyed our play.

My class came out on stage to take a bow. The audience stood up and cheered.

On the way out of the auditorium, they filled our penny jar to the brim. We were gigundoly proud.

Here Comes the Parade

We had fun with the winter carnival all week. We went sledding and ice-skating. We walked up and down our street selling brownies we had baked ourselves. (Well, Mommy helped a little. And we did *not* have any fires.)

Then on Saturday morning Ms. Feld had a winter story hour at the library. She read us winter chapters from different books.

In the afternoon, Hannie, Nancy, and I entered a snow-art festival. We made three snow angels holding hands. They looked like paper dolls made of snow. We named our work of art "The Three Musketeers" and we each went home with a red ribbon.

The week had flown by. Seth had called every night. He still had not made a decision about the job. He said we could keep talking about it. Then early Sunday morning, he came home. Andrew and I threw our arms around him.

"You made it!" I said.

"I sure did," said Seth. "And I am so happy to see you."

At noon Mommy, Seth, Andrew, and I drove downtown. It felt good to have my little-house family together.

In the town square, I looked for Natalie. I had not seen her much after school. That is because the Snow Prince and Snow Princess had winter-carnival meetings to attend.

"Greetings, citizens of Stoneybrook!" said Mayor Keane.

She was standing at the podium in the town square. "This parade is the last event in our weeklong winter carnival. The carni-

94

val has been a great success, and we thank you all for taking part. Enjoy!"

We heard a drumroll. Then a marching band started down the street. The band was followed by four huge floats heading toward the square.

On the very first float I saw Natalie, dressed as the Snow Princess, waving her wand. Bill Korman, the Snow Prince, was by her side.

I was gigundoly proud and happy for my friend. I had pushed her into the contest, but it was her own composition that had won. Natalie Springer, whose socks were always drooping and who was shy in front of crowds, was princess for a week. This was a very good thing for her to be.

I jumped up and down and waved my arms so Natalie could see me. (I wished I had worn my yellow sweater and lights.) "Hi, Natalie!" I called as she passed by.

She turned to me and smiled.

When the float reached the square, the Snow Prince and Snow Princess climbed down. I was not sure what was going to happen next. Natalie and Bill seemed to have a special job to do.

The deputy mayor handed them a giant envelope. Natalie and Bill each held one corner. Then they stepped up to the podium where the mayor was waiting.

"On behalf of the town of Stoneybrook, we present this check to you," said Bill.

"There is money for a new fire truck and enough left over to help make our town more beautiful," said Natalie.

I could hardly believe it. Natalie did not trip up on her words. She spoke loudly and clearly. She looked like a real and true princess.

Then Natalie and Bill turned and smiled at the crowd. Camera lights were flashing as news reporters snapped their pictures.

I caught Natalie's eye and gave her the thumbs-up sign. Natalie waved her wand at me. She was beaming. And so was I.

L. GODWIN

About the Author

Ann M. Martin lives in New York City and loves animals, especially cats. She has two cats of her own, Gussie and Woody.

Other books by Ann M. Martin that you might enjoy are *Stage Fright*; *Me and Katie (the Pest)*; and the books in *The Baby-sitters Club* series.

Ann likes ice cream and *I Love Lucy*. And she has her own little sister, whose name is Jane.

Little Sister

Don't miss #95

KAREN'S PROMISE

Daddy nodded. "We did not want to take you away from your friends and school in the middle of the term like this. That is why we thought it would be best if you made this decision yourself."

I nodded. I felt proud that everyone trusted me enough to make this decision on my own. But it was a gigundoly big decision.

I looked over at Andrew. He kept staring at me. I knew he wanted me to tell everyone I was going to Chicago with him. But I needed to think some more. I sighed. This was not going to be easy.

Little Sister

by Ann M. Martin
author of The Baby-sitters Club®

More Titles... ➡

LITTLE 🍎 APPLE®

Here are some of our favorite Little Apples.

There are fun times ahead with kids just like you in Little Apple books! Once you take a bite out of a Little Apple—you'll want to read more!

Reading Excitement for Kids with BIG Appetites!

☐ NA45899-X **Amber Brown Is Not a Crayon**
Paula Danziger $2.99

☐ NA93425-2 **Amber Brown Goes Fourth**
Paula Danziger $2.99

☐ NA50207-7 **You Can't Eat Your Chicken Pox, Amber Brown**
Paula Danziger $2.99

☐ NA42833-0 **Catwings** Ursula K. LeGuin $2.95

☐ NA42832-2 **Catwings Return** Ursula K. LeGuin $3.50

☐ NA41821-1 **Class Clown** Johanna Hurwitz $2.99

☐ NA42400-9 **Five True Horse Stories**
Margaret Davidson $2.99

☐ NA43868-9 **The Haunting of Grade Three**
Grace Maccarone $2.99

☐ NA40966-2 **Rent a Third Grader** B.B. Hiller $2.99

☐ NA41944-7 **The Return of the Third Grade Ghost Hunters**
Grace Maccarone $2.99

☐ NA42031-3 **Teacher's Pet** Johanna Hurwitz $3.50

Available wherever you buy books...or use the coupon below.

- -

SCHOLASTIC INC., P.O. Box 7502, 2931 East McCarty Street, Jefferson City, MO 65102

Please send me the books I have checked above. I am enclosing $ _____ (please add $2.00 to cover shipping and handling). Send check or money order—no cash or C.O.D.s please.

Name_____

Address_____

City_____State/Zip_____

Please allow four to six weeks for delivery. Offer good in the U.S.A. only. Sorry, mail orders are not available to residents of Canada. Prices subject to change.   LA996